VERY HAIRY HARRY

By Edward Koren

JOANNA COTLER BOOKS
An Imprint of HarperCollins*Publishers*

W9-APH-075

To the memory of my father, Harry Koren, and my chum Tom Winship, neither very hairy. —E.K.

Very Hairy Harry Copyright © 2003 by Edward Koren Printed in the U.S.A. All rights reserved. www.harperchildrens.com
Library of Congress Cataloging-in-Publication Data Koren, Edward. Very hairy Harry / by Edward Koren.— 1st ed.   p. cm. Summary: Harry learns the advantages and disadvantages of being really hairy.
ISBN 0-06-050907-4 — ISBN 0-06-050908-2 (lib. bdg.) [1. Hair—Fiction.] I. Title. PZ7.K83647 Ve 2003 [E]—dc21 2002011311 Typography by Alicia Mikles 1 2 3 4 5 6 7 8 9 10 ❖ First Edition

Hey, Harry!
I hear you want
to be HAIRY.

Would you like to be a little

HAIRIER, Harry?

HAIRIER than anybody else?

Maybe you'd like to see yourself really HAIRY!

So HAIRY, Harry,

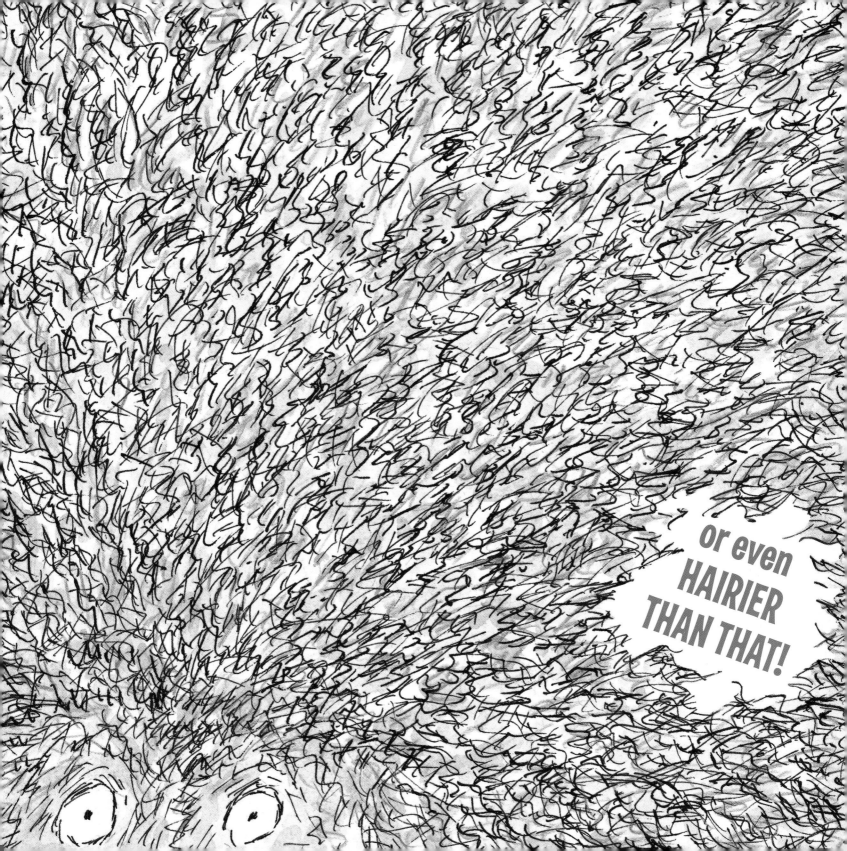

or even
HAIRIER
THAN THAT!

Hairy means:

Your dog can look like he's a part of you,

and your cat can
sit in your shade.

Hairy means:
You can play

-AND-

without moving.

Hairy means:

The other team will NEVER find the ball.

AND you can keep warm without your jacket, snow pants, hat, mittens, scarf, earmuffs, socks, or boots!

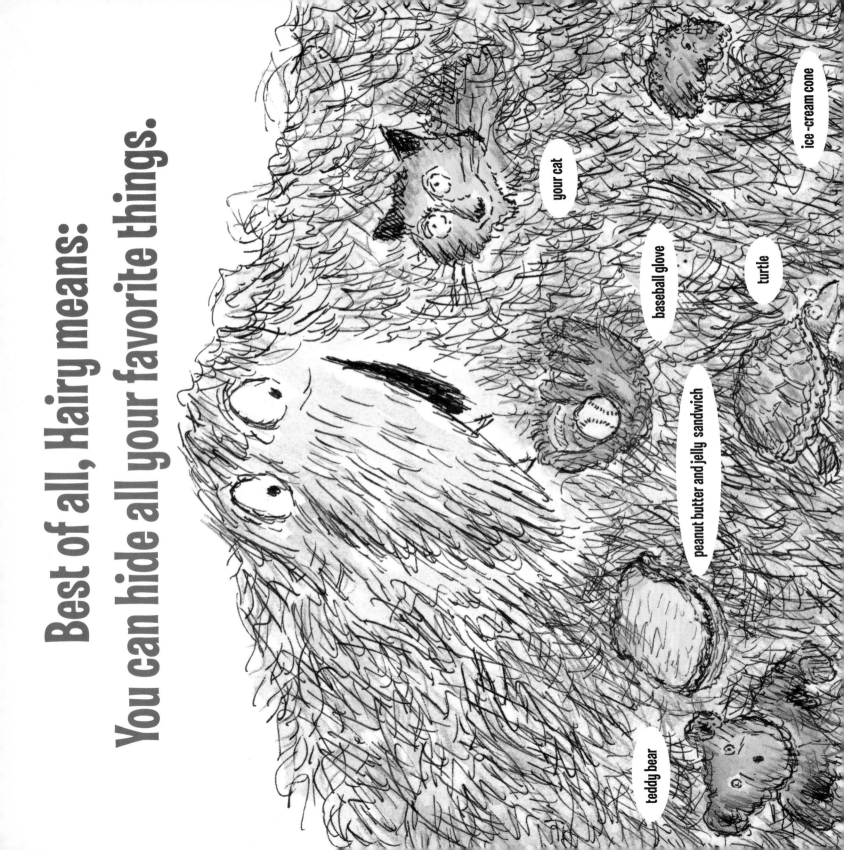

Best of all, Hairy means:
You can hide all your favorite things.

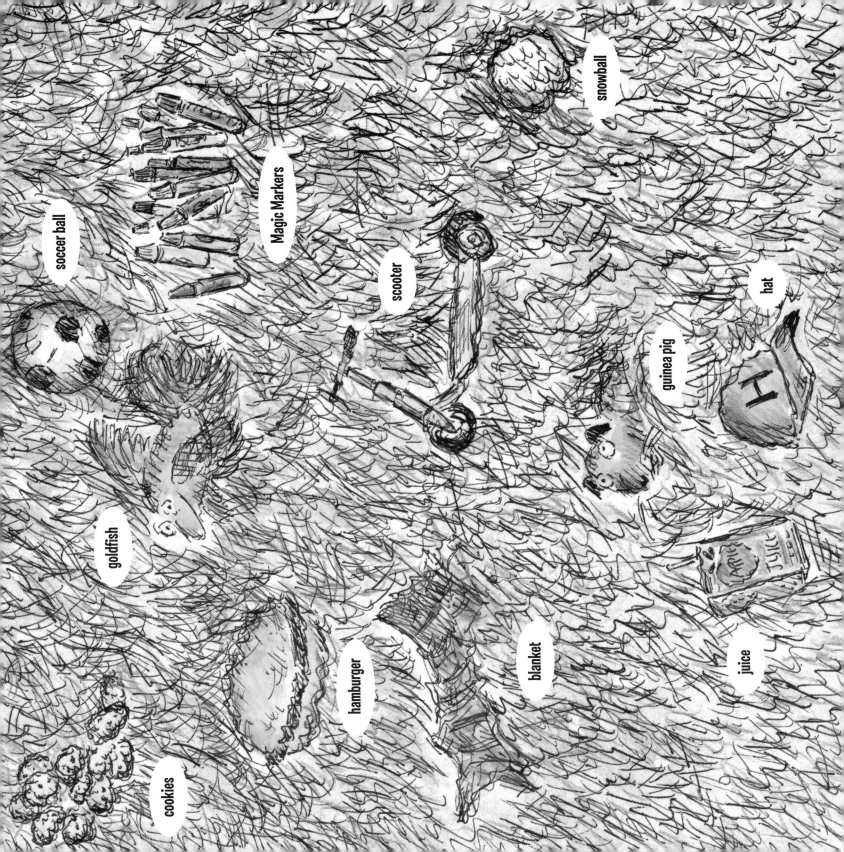

means that you

Happier now, Harry?